AF408764

OUTLAWS PUBLISHING

DRIFTER

JOHN THURMOND

For information contact: info@outlawspublishing.com

Cover Art by Michael Thomas
Cover design by Outlaws Publishing
Published by Outlaws Publishing
April 2021
10987654321

Chapter 1

Ranger Beacher Tolbert nearly blew himself up when he and Ranger Joe Tolbert, a first cousin, dropped two or three sticks of dynamite down in the roof of a cave, with little more than a crack in the ceiling. The roof fell right on top of some outlaws they had been chasing. Beacher had turned to run, tripped and fell, nearly blowing himself up. He'd flown up in the air, losing a boot, and fell into the cavern himself. Ranger Joe Tolbert had to pull him out and told everyone he met for a month after it happened, still laughing about the sight.

Years later, Ranger Tolbert, teacher and lawman, had been sitting in a classroom at a place called Baylor in Waco, Texas, off and on for three years trying to teach some bone-head lawmen and soon to be Justices of the Peace, along with would-be Judges, enough about what they could and could not do according to Texas law.

It was late in the afternoon and Beacher was thinking to himself. "Is this all I'm going to do for the rest of my life?" He walked to his favorite cantina. It had a big sign outside that read "Rose's" hung over the boardwalk. He pulled his .45 and put two holes after "Rose's." He hadn't fired a gun in three years and it sure felt good.

Waco Sheriff, Mack Boyles, walked up behind him. "Beacher, you know we got a city ordinance against firing a gun inside the city limits."

"Yeah, I wrote it. What about it?" Beacher asked.

"Nothing," Mack said. "Come on, I'll buy you a beer." If Mack had ever learned anything about Beacher Tolbert, it was that if the man was in a bad mood, leave him the hell alone.

Beacher stayed in Rose's until the moon came out, then walked to the boarding house and turned in. He laid there all night, looking at the ceiling. It had the little, metal, square, designer plates with small nails around the edges. He found one that had more nails than the others and laid there wondering why.

Beacher was up before sunrise, sitting in a local café. He was on his third cup of coffee when he made a decision to send Austin a wire that read, "Ranger Beacher Tolbert, taking some time off. Just going to ride out west and look around some. Will wire you when I'm done." He ordered himself a big breakfast, something he hadn't done in a long time. After he was finished, he walked to the livery and made a deal for the tallest and longest-legged horse, the biggest in Waco. It was a big Tennessee Walker, close to sixteen hands high. Beacher still had his old saddle and bags, so he packed extra clothes and his bed roll in a new tarp. With enough food to last for a week, the Ranger left Waco, Texas for the first time in three years.

Beacher had taken to carrying his badge in a leather folder, along with his folding money. As he rode out of Waco he was thinking, "I'm just going to drift around for a while. I'm riding west with the morning sun at my back, not thinking about anything but the world around me. I haven't done that since leaving Illinois. Man, that seems like a hundred years ago."

Thinking of Illinois started Beacher to thinking about the last dance he had gone to, and all the trouble he had gotten into. A bully had pushed him off the dance floor, nearly knocking him out. Beacher had sneaked up behind the bully and whacked him across the top of his head with a pole axe. That had cost Tolbert a week in the Jefferson County jail. He started thinking of the girl he had danced with. "Get her out of your mind," he thought. "You didn't care much for her anyway."

Beacher drifted on past the Leon River and stopped at a little place near there called Gatesville. He had dinner in a café and rode on west. Dark found the Ranger at the Lampasas River. It was wider and had more water than the Leon. He made camp, and he didn't want company. He knew he would run into the Colorado River before noon the next day. Or, at least, the maps he carried showed that he should. Some of the Texas Rangers that Tolbert had been teaching the law had talked about catfish as big as a man in the Colorado River, just north of where it met up with the Llano River. Tolbert had the idea of catching one. "I haven't had fish to fry since I was kid back home," he thought.

It took Beacher longer than he figured to find the Colorado River. By the time he made camp, the sun was at the west back. "Just right," he said to himself. He cut some bank poles and found some toad frogs. "The smaller ones work better," Beacher thought. "Now all I need are some hooks and line, with no weights. Just run your hook under the frog's backbone near his hind legs, and he won't bleed a bit. He'll swim toward the bank all night." Tolbert knew that the forked-tail catfish was a top feeder, unlike the round-tail, yellow catfish which fed off the bottom.

Beacher set his poles and finished his camp site. He places rocks in a circle for a fire and hug his tarp in case it rained, which was unlikely for west Texas. He built a small fire, just big enough to make coffee, and had dried beef to chew on with some old bread. He staked his horse out in the grass at the edge of the water, had some coffee, and turned in an hour or so after dark.

A catfish flopping in the water on the end of a line, woke the Ranger up. He shook his boots out and pulled them on. He saw a small boy or girl around the age of eight years or so, in the water trying to pull in a big catfish. Beacher looked around and saw the kid was alone and his fire was out. The kid had not seen his camp, just the fish on a bank pole. He watched to be sure the little kid was going to be able to pull the fish in, as the fish looked to be larger than the kid was. The kid managed to pull the fish up on the bank far enough that it wouldn't be able to flop back into the water.

"The kid is pretty smart," Beacher thought. He grabbed the kid by an overall strap, picking it up. The kid was a she, and she screamed.

"Hold on," he said. "I'm not going to hurt you. I just wanted to know who you are, since you're stealing my fish."

"Ain't your fish," she said, "I drug him in."

Beacher sat the girl down. "Yeah, but it's on my hook," he said.

She responded with, "You got poof it's your hook? Does it have your name on it? No, it don't. In Texas possession is nine tenths of the law." She stood there and stared the Ranger down.

Beacher was thinking, "This lid might know more about the law than some of them bone-head Rangers I've been teaching."

"How about we fry him up and you can have half?" he asked the girl.

"Okay," she said, "But you get to clean him, too."

So, there was Beacher Tolbert, Texas Ranger, cleaning a fish that must have weighed ten pounds, around midnight. The little girl got the fire going again and they had a fish fry. They caught three more fish before morning.

"Tell me about yourself," Beacher told the little girl.

"No, you first," she said. "My mom said I was not to talk to strangers. If you tell me who you are, we won't be strangers anymore."

So there sat Beacher Tolbert, telling a little girl who he was. Her eyes were as big as eggs as she listened to his life history. Of course, Beacher threw in a tall tale or two.

"Wow," she said, "You can lie better than any of the boys in my school.

Beacher showed her his Ranger badge.

"All of that was the truth?" she asked.

"Yes, it's all true," Beacher said with his fingers crossed behind his back.

She just stared at the man. For an eight-year-old she was pretty smart. As the sun was coming up, she asked if she could have a fish to take home. Beacher got her a big one, ran a stick through his gills and mouth so she could carry it. She started across the river, which was only waist deep on her.

"What's your name?" Beacher called out.

"Katy," she called back. "And you're?"

"Beacher," the Ranger replied.

"Good-bye, Beacher," she sang out, and she was gone.

Beacher camped two more days in the same place and never saw Katy again. "She must be raiding someone else's fishing pole," he thought.

Chapter 2

Beacher had wasted a week fishing and never caught anything bigger than ten pounds. Finally, breaking camp, he rode to Bluffton, a small town on the west side of the Colorado River. It looked to be around a quarter mile from the river bluff on the west side, overlooking the river for nearly half a mile. Tired of his own cooking, Beacher went to the local café. He found a table next to the kitchen and saw Katy waiting on customers. "The café must belong to her folks," he thought.

Katy came around to his table. "What do you want to eat, Beacher?" she asked. She instantly put her hand over her mouth. Her mother saw the interaction from the kitchen window.

"Why did you call that man Beacher?" her mother asked.

"He's a Texas Ranger," Katy said, "And he knows how to fish. He had the biggest fish I ever saw on a hook and I dragged it in."

"So," Beacher said, "You finally admit that it was my fish and not yours."

"Well," Katy replied, "I dragged him in. All you did with that hook was slow him down some."

The two had a staring contest going on. Beacher wasn't going to give up and it looked as if she was going to win. He finally gave up when her mother brought out the steak and eggs he'd ordered.

"Just where did you two meet?" she asked.

Beacher wasn't going to tell because he didn't want to get the little girl into trouble. Besides, he was busy eating. He pointed his fork at Katy and said, "Tell your mom."

Katy set in to telling the biggest tall tale Beacher had ever heard, about her pulling a big catfish out of the river and him claiming it was his just because of the hook in its mouth. Beacher could see this was never going to be settled, that it would be an ongoing feud between himself and Katy. Finally, he said, "I'm Beacher Tolbert, Texas Ranger." Her mother introduced herself as Miss Viola Haldeman.

"Don't tell anyone I'm a Texas Ranger," Tolbert said. "Keep it to yourself." The mother and child agreed. Viola was a good-looking woman, but Beacher kept that to himself.

Beacher decided to hang around Bluffton. It looked like every town in Texas and had everything you'd need to ranch. There was even a small hotel and a boarding house. He rented a room at the boarding the house because it looked cleaner than the hotel.

He was hanging out in the cantina, listening to some cowhands talking about a stranger named Red Clawson who was moving in and taking over some of the smaller ranches. Beacher was wondering if the man was doing this legally or by force. His curiosity got the better of him and he finally asked the cowhands, "What ranches has this Red Clawson bought out so far?"

"Well," one hand answered, "He bought Jack Webber, our boss, out and he's already left the country. Then there was a small horse rancher just across the river from the Webber Ranch, I believe his name was Danny Haldeman."

Beacher bought the men a beer and listened to the small talk for the rest of the day. He decided to check the land deeds at the courthouse the following day. There was a land warranty deed on Jack Webber, but the signature was a lot older than ten years before. Tolbert knew that people's handwriting changed with age, but never for the better. The signature on the land deed looked as though whoever signed it was trying hard. The same thing was present on a deed for Dan Haldeman.

"I wonder if he's kin to Viola and Katy," Beacher thought. "I need to find out."

Beacher saw some cowhands sitting in the shade outside the cantina on the boardwalk. He asked to sit and talked with them a while. He learned they were brothers, Chuck and Ted Younger.

"I'm Beacher Tolbert," he introduced himself.

Chuck stared at Tolbert for a while and said, "You're that Texas Ranger from over at Waco. The one that dropped a stick of dynamite down the crack in a cave roof and brought it down on top of a bunch of outlaws. You nearly blew yourself up and fell in the hole."

"Yes, that's me, but keep it to yourself," Beacher said. Hell, every cowboy in the country was still laughing about that. "There's something here I'm looking into."

"Okay," Chuck said.

"If we can help, let us know. We used to work on the Webber spread. Old man Webber sold out and left town, still owing us wages," Ted said.

"Did he tell you he sold out, or did Red Clawson tell you?" Beacher asked.

"Well, Clawson came around and told us weren't needed there anymore and laid us off."

"So, you never saw Jack Webber after the ranch was sold?" asked the Ranger.

"No, he just left town."

"Do you know anybody who saw him leave?"

"No," both brothers said.

"Do you have time to show me his fence line?" Beacher asked.

"Sure, we'd be glad to," Chuck said.

"It's too late in the day," Beacher replied. "Let's start first thing in the morning. I'll meet you at the café come daylight."

Beacher was already waiting there when the Younger brothers showed up. They just ordered coffee. Ted was staring at Beacher's plate.

"The Texas Rangers are paying for a meal if you're hungry," he told the two. Both Ted and Chuck ordered and cleaned their plates out. Not a crumb was left. Beacher was thinking to himself, "These boys are broke or down to their last dollar. A lot of cowboys turn to rustling when they're broke. It's starve or survive."

The Webber Ranch was south of town nearly ten miles. It ran along the Llano River on the east back for about six or seven miles, then east to an old bluff called Marble Falls. Beacher could see a lot of buzzards flying around in the air a mile on farther north and decided to check it out. He'd seen a mountain lion when he was fishing and wondered if it was a fresh kill.

"Let's check it out, Chuck," Beacher told the cowboy.

They rode up on a scene that was hard to describe. The buzzards and other vermin had done a good job of cleaning up both a horse and its rider. A saddle, boots and guns were the only things left besides bones. Beacher and the cowboys sat a while, taking in the grizzly scene.

"We better check under the saddle," Beacher said. "A lot of times men will brand their names on the underside. Helps against theft, and in times like this."

Tolbert cut the belly strap, pulled the saddle off to one side, and turned it over. J. Webber was branded as plain as day. The three men stayed at the site the rest of the day, covering the skeletons with rocks. Beacher took his Ranger handbook and made an entry of what they had found, the date of the tenth day of July 1884, and an approximate location in guessing how far north of Marble Falls they were, in case some of Webber's kin folks started looking for him. Beacher decided to wire Austin with his suspicion of foul play, and to see if he could deputize the Younger brothers.

Tolbert wired Austin a short note from Lampasas that read, "A man named Red Clawson from back east taking over. Two ranches so far. Found one former owner as buzzard bait, along with his horse. Land deed signature does not match a Jack Webber. Checking on another rancher now. Request permission to deputize two former hands of Webber ranch, Chuck and Ted Younger, ASAP. Both good men. Hold here for answer."

The Ranger and the cowboys were in the cantina when the sheriff brought the response wire. Beacher motioned for the sheriff to sit down. Tolbert read the note from Austin. The response said, "Will check for Red Clawson name on wanted list. Deputize men and pay out of your pocket. Expense will be reimbursed to you."

Tolbert looked at the sheriff and asked, "Do you have any deputy badges?"

"Sure," the sheriff replied, "How many do you need?"

"Two."

The men walked over to the sheriff's office and Beacher swore the Younger brothers into service. He borrowed paper and pen and wrote their names along with their duties and had both men sign.

"You said you wanted to help," Beacher told his new deputies, "I figured you're both broke or close to it. The job pays twenty dollars a month plus expenses. Keep up with what you spend in the line of service only."

Beacher paid the men in advance. "You'd have thought I'd given them a fortune," he thought.

"Let's see about the Haldeman spread," the Ranger said. "Either of you know anything about his ranch?"

"It's just a one-man spread, is what I've heard," Chuck said. "He owned the west side of Llano River across from the Webber place. That gives Clawson control of the river."

"Well," Beacher told him, "I looked at the deed at the courthouse. Danny Haldeman's hand writing was like Webber's, it didn't match up with the originals on file. What do you boys know about Haldeman?"

"I heard he came in here by himself and filed on his spread," Ted said. "Just about thirty-six hundred acres three years ago, along the west side of the Llano River. He only had saddle horses. He built a barn and shack under some trees along the river bank. That's about all I know about him."

"What about the Haldeman woman who runs the café?" Beacher asked.

"It hasn't been open long, maybe a couple of months. Now that I'm thinking about it, she showed up after Danny Haldeman sold out," Chuck said.

"Well, she did tell me she was Miss Haldeman," Beacher replied. "I better ask."

Chapter 3

At the café the next morning Beacher asked Viola if she knew Danny Haldeman. She sat down at the table with him and the Younger brothers and just stared at the Ranger.

"Yes, he's my older brother," she said. "I haven't seen him in a year. He asked me to come out west on the stage. He was supposed to meet me here in Bluffton, but he never showed up. I had just enough money to go back to Mississippi or start this café. If me and Katy went back, we would have had nothing, no home or kin folks. It was either stay here or starve back home. We stayed. You're the first person to mention Danny's name since we've been here. Why are you asking about Danny?"

"These brothers, Chuck and Ted Younger, are now my deputies," Beacher began. "They were laid off from the Jack Webber spread after he sold out. But, we found his body, along with his horse, up in the hills. The buzzards had just about cleaned him up, and we identified him by the name branded under his saddle. A man named Red Clawson claims to have bought him out, but the signatures on the deeds are not a match. It's the same with Danny's deed, not a match. I don't think it would hold up in court if you wanted to claim his ranch. It's not very big, but worth enough to fight for. I can file a court case and make a claim for you. At least we may find out what happened to Danny. We will have to file in

Lampasas, it's the only town around with a courthouse and a sheriff. The Texas Rangers will file your claim. If someone asks you about Danny or a court case, tell them nothing. I have no idea what kind of man this Red Clawson is."

Beacher told the Younger brothers to hide their badges and just hang around town. He said he wanted one of the deputies in the café at all time. "It's not very big, so wash dishes or clean tables," he told them. "Keep yourself low profile and your ears open. I'm going over to Lampasas and file a court case against Red Clawson, on behalf of Danny Haldeman and Jack Webber. While it's on my mind, Ted, you go back and get Webber's saddle. Take it to the Lampasas livery barn and hide it in the loft. Tell the stable boy where it's at and to leave it alone until a Texas Ranger asks for it. We may have need of it during court."

Tolbert rode to Lampasas the following day to see Sheriff James Dun. He told the sheriff what he'd found and about Jack Webber and his horse. He asked the sheriff if he knew Red Clawson.

"Never heard of him," the sheriff replied.

"Well, I'm going to file a fraud case against him for Danny Haldeman's next of kin, and on Jack Webber's ranch for unpaid back wages. The land deed filing signatures don't match up and Danny has disappeared. I'm filing on behalf of his sister."

Beacher walked over to the courthouse and filed all the correct papers, and personally delivered them to the local judge.

"Who's going to be Danny Haldeman's kin folks' lawyer?" the judge asked.

"I am. Beacher Tolbert, Texas Ranger."

"You can't do that," the judge said, "You're no lawyer."

"Judge, you need to wire Austin now or I am going to replace you with someone who's a lot smarter than you are," Beacher responded.

This made the judge mad and he wired Austin. The judge saw Beacher later at the cantina and all he could say was, "Mister Tolbert." The Ranger told him to shut up and that if he ever called him "Mister" again, he'd be shot in the backside.

Beacher also saw Ted in the cantina, who only nodded and whispered, "It's done."

The court date was set for thirty days from then. Either the sheriff or a Texas Ranger had to give Red Clawson notice within three days from the filing date. Beacher told both the judge and the sheriff that he would be the one to give Red Clawson notice of the court date.

The Ranger got both Chuck and Ted to ride with him because they knew the Webber spread and Beacher was sure Red would have made it his headquarters as Danny's place only had a two-room shack.

The Webber house and corrals, along with a small barn and bunkhouse, sat in a valley. The whole spread could be seen from the top of the ridge. Beacher counted six horses and a buggy. Someone was sitting on the porch when the Ranger and his deputies rode up. The man got up, walked to a post, and stayed there until Beacher and his men stopped.

The first thing out the stranger's mouth was, "Who are you and what the hell do you want?"

Beacher knew that if this was Red Clawson, he was going to enjoy serving papers on the man.

"You Red Clawson?" Beacher asked.

"Yea," Clawson answered. He had red hair and a mustache. Beacher could see why they called him Red.

"I'm Texas Ranger Beacher Tolbert," he said as he handed Clawson the papers, "Be in Lampasas Court House twenty-three days from today. That's a Monday, if you have a calendar. Bring proof of purchase on the land deal you made with Danny Haldeman. The deed is being contested by the next of kin on behalf of Danny Haldeman. If you're not there the court will side with the Haldeman family members and you will have two days to vacate the property."

Red Clawson yelled, "Get the hell off my property right now!"

Beacher replied, "You don't know much about Texas Law, Red. Being a Texas Ranger gives me the right to go anywhere I want to, anytime I want to, day or night. Now, unless you would like to stay in jail until this court date, I would shut the hell up."

Red went back to his rocker and never said another word. "Dang," he said to himself, "Hadn't planned for no Texas Ranger sticking his nose into my business."

Beacher looked at Chuck and said, "Show me around some," as they rode off. "I'd like to see the Llano River near the Haldeman place."

Danny had built his cabin close to where the Colorado and Llano Rivers met. There were a lot of big trees and shade. He had the perfect place for a horse ranch, with good water and grass. Beacher could see why Red wanted it, along with the Webber spread. He asked Chuck if Jack Webber had any next of kin that he knew of.

"None I ever heard of," Chuck said.

"What about you, Ted?" Beacher asked. "You know of any?"

"None that Jack ever talked about. We worked for him for close to five years," Ted replied.

"Were you paid up on wages?" the Ranger asked.

"No, Jack still owed us our winter wages. He was waiting on the spring sale of calves. Why?" Chuck asked Beacher.

"Let me think on it until the Haldeman case is settled," Beacher told him.

As they rode up to Danny's cabin, a man came out with a rifle.

"Texas Ranger," Beacher identified himself. "These other men are my deputies. Tell me who you are."

"Butch Chania," the man said. "Why?"

"This the Haldeman spread?" asked Beacher.

"No, it belongs to Red Clawson."

"How long have you known Red?"

"A couple of months," Butch said.

"Do you know a Danny Haldeman?" Beacher asked.

"Never heard of him," Butch replied. "Why?"

"Well, the Haldeman family members are suing Red Clawson to get this place back," Tolbert told him. "If you've been paid stay, if not, I would get out of here because you're never going to get paid. The Haldeman family has an iron-clad case that will be impossible for them to lose."

Butch walked out to his horse and left.

"Trail him, Ted," Beacher said, "See where he goes."

Ted waited until Butch left and trailed him all the way to Fredericksburg. When Ted saw Beacher the following morning, he told the Ranger where Butch had gone.

"Looks like he left the country," Beacher remarked. "Something about this whole set up is not making a lot of sense."

"Why?" Chuck asked.

"Well, Red doesn't have any hands. Butch just ups and leaves when I tell him he may not get paid," Beacher explained. "What would you or Ted do if I rode up and told you you're not getting paid? You would have ridden over to see Red and asked him."

"Yeah, I would have," Chuck said. "Not just leave the country. You're right, it doesn't make sense when you think about it."

Chapter 4

After the Civil War came to an end, Red Clawson and some men of the Confederate unit he was in got separated from their unit and began wandering around, trying to hide from the Union Army. The men started stealing from anyone they came across, even Southern families. They burned anything in their way and killed a lot of people. Even though they knew the war had ended, they just kept on stealing and killing until the Federal Union started hunting them down. A lot of the men were hung for stealing pigs and chickens. A small number of them headed west through Arkansas, the Indian Territory, and drifted down into Texas. They had in mind to join up with Quantrill's Raiders, as they had heard that he and some men were going down into Mexico to join up with Benito Juarez.

By the time Red made it all the way to Texas, Quantrill was already dead. Of course, Red didn't know that. He was following the river south and found that nearly all the river bottom land was settled on. He knew that if you couldn't get water, you weren't going to raise anything. He followed the Colorado River down to where it met up with the Llano and felt that this was his place. He talked Danny Haldeman into letting him help around the spread for a meal while helping to build a small horse barn. The job lasted nearly two weeks. When Danny told

Red he was through, Red pulled his gun and killed the man.

Red was tired of men telling him what to do. He rolled Danny's body into the river and watched him float downstream. The water was higher than usual. The next day, Red drove all of Danny's horses to Fredericksburg and sold them at the livery barn as unbroken stock. He told the porter there that he had too many to break by himself. Taking part of the money, Red got a needed shave and bath, with new duds to put on. He went drinking and spending money at the Black Horse Cantina. There Red Clawson spotted an old comrade, Butch Chania. He told Butch that he had a place of his own and how he had acquired it.

Red and Butch got roaring drunk that night. Red talked Butch into going back with him. After looking the place over Red suggested, "Let's go to the courthouse and change his deed. No one in the country knows other ranchers, they're too far apart."

Clawson got the county clerk at the courthouse to make out a warranty deed and Butch signed it as Danny Haldeman. They went back to the Black Horse Cantina and bought a beer. "Damn," Red told Butch, "That was easy. I bet you we could get the Webber place just as easy. The old man has a ranch just across the river on the east side of the Llano. It's different country, and Jack Webber is an old man. Haldeman told me Webber had no kin folks, his wife passed away, and there are no kids to bother us. We could just shoot him, fire his hands and move on in. Who's going to stop us? After we're there for a year we'll just sell the place and his cattle off to the highest bidder."

The two men began watching Webber, hiding in the tree line east of Jack's ranch. Nearly a month passed before they finally caught the old man on the Far East side of the ranch by himself, north of Marble Falls.

"Butch, shoot his horse so he can't run off, then go home," Clawson said. "I'll take care of Webber." Red waited until he heard Butch's gun and then pulled the trigger on his own rifle.

They left the dead man there with his horse and rode straight to Lampasas and filed a new deed. Butch signed his name as Jack Webber and the deed was done. Red and Butch then rode out to the ranch and laid off Webber's hands, being just the two Younger brothers. Red told the brothers that Jack had sold out and they weren't needed anymore. Red found that there was only enough food stock for the winter. "Man," he was thinking, "We got it made. Now we can sit a while and sell out next year." Clawson thought it was easy money, until the damned Ranger showed up.

After Beacher and the Younger brothers left, Red rode over to Danny's place. The horse droppings in the corral were old. "Butch must have left out when the Ranger showed up," Red thought. "I better ride over to Fredericksburg and find him."

Butch was in the same cantina as before. Red asked him why he left.

"Texas Ranger and two other men showed up," Butch told him. "Said the land deed was being contested by family members and there was no way they could lose the case. No need for me to hang around and go to jail. Hell, all I done was shoot Webber's horse. You can count me out of this deal right now."

This made Red mad and he started to pull his gun. Butch beat him to the draw. He already had his own gun out and just stuck it in Red's face. "Get out of town," Butch told Clawson. "The next time I see you I'm just going to start shooting." Red left Fredericksburg. He needed to find out who was kin to Danny Haldeman.

Beacher got to worrying about why Butch would just leave and not ask Red for his pay, or any pay at all. Fredericksburg wasn't very far.

"I think I'm going to ask Butch," Beacher announced. "Ted, you stay in Bluffton and watch the café."

Beacher rode into Fredericksburg and started looking for Butch Chania. He finally found the man in the Black Horse Cantina, leaning on the bar and talking to some other men. He had a beer in his right hand. Just inside the swinging doors Beacher said aloud, "Butch, I need to talk to you about Red Clawson."

"Damn, that was fast," thought Butch. He pulled his pistol with his left hand. He wore it on his right side, backwards with the grips facing forward. Beating the Ranger to the draw, he had his gun up and fanned the hammer back with is right hand, firing a shot before Beacher cleared leather with his own gun. The Ranger felt his hat fly off before he ever pulled the trigger. Butch fired two more rounds before Beacher's shot hit him dead center. The impact slammed Butch back into the bar, then he pitched forward and hit the floor face down with dust flying up all around him. He was dead. Beacher retrieved his hat, which had a big hole in the brim. Butch had hit the Ranger's hat, broken a window and a chair about a foot away.

The sheriff showed up and demanded, "What's going on in here?"

Beacher showed the sheriff his badge.

"You need to wear that out in the front," the sheriff commented.

"I wear it where I want to," Beacher said. "Let's walk over to your office, we need to talk in private." Once the door was closed, Beacher introduced himself to Sheriff Pat Buchanan and told him what was going on.

"Damn," Buchanan said, "I was wondering why I haven't heard from Jack Webber in a while."

"You kin to him?" Beacher asked.

"No, just friends," the sheriff said.

"Do you know of any kin folks Jack had?"

"No, he just had a wife, but she passed some time back," Buchanan said. "Al little over a year or so ago."

"Well," Beacher said, "Jack owed back wages to the Younger brothers, Chuck and Ted. If Jack has no kin, then I may assign his estate over into the care of them for ten years. If no claim in made on the estate by then, you can sign the deed in a Sheriff's sale, and all they will owe is the taxes."

Beacher rode back to Bluffton, getting there late. Everything in town was closed, but he didn't feel he could eat anyway. He was still wound up over the shootout with Butch. He went to his room at the boarding house and tried to sleep. "Damn, he was fast," Beacher was thinking as he lay there. "I did not realize his gun was in its holster backwards. I saw the beer in his right hand, but he fooled me when he drew his gun with his left hand before I could blink. The only mistake he made was fanning his gun. That's never very accurate, but he did manage to put a round in my hat. Good thing I'm only five feet ten inches." The Ranger did not sleep well.

Unknown to Beacher, Red Clawson was trying to find Haldeman's next of kin. He had asked every person in Bluffton before the blacksmith said, "I believe the woman who runs the café's last name is Haldeman. Yeah, Viola Haldeman, I believe. Why you asking?" the smithy inquired.

"I've got a message from Danny Haldeman," Red told him. "A private matter."

"Yeah?" the blacksmith asked. "I heard he sold out."

Red just rode away and went to the café. He was sitting there eating breakfast when Ted Younger came in. Ted saw Clawson and ignored the outlaw as he walked to a corner table and sat down. Ted watched the man until he left then asked Viola, "Is that all he wanted, just breakfast? Did he ask your name?"

"No," Viola said. "Just breakfast. No talking at all."

"That was Red Clawson," Ted told her. "He has his name on Danny Haldeman's place."

"You think he's hunting me down?" Viola asked. "Because of the lawsuit against the deed?"

"Why else would he be prowling around?" Ted offered. "I need to tell Beacher."

Just then Beacher walked into the café. Ted told him, "Red just left."

"What did he want?" Beacher asked.

"Just breakfast is all," Ted remarked.

"Did he ride off or walk?" asked the Ranger.

"He rode off."

Beacher walked outside. The sun was just above the river. The only fresh horse tracks coming to the café came from the direction of the blacksmith shop. The tracks going away went downtown. Beacher walked to the blacksmith.

"Has anybody been asking about Danny Haldeman's kin folks this morning?" he asked the smithy.

"Depends on who's asking," the blacksmith replied.

Tolbert showed his badge.

"Yeah, a big feller, had red hair all over him," the blacksmith said. "I watched him ride to the café. I told him a Miss Viola Haldeman ran the place."

"That was Red Clawson," Beacher replied. "An outlaw, I believe."

"Well, he won't get any more information out of me," the smithy swore.

Chapter 5

Red saw one of the Younger boys, Ted he thought was his name, when he walked into the café and found himself a table. Red finished his meal and left. He was going to have a talk with Viola Haldeman, but with one of Webber's hands around, decided against it. Clawson rode downtown, circled around and hid in the alley across from the café, watching and trying to figure out what to do about the Haldeman woman. He stayed there until sundown. A small girl came skipping down the boardwalk and stopped in front of the café just as a man came out. "Is my momma still in there?" he overheard her ask. "Yes," the man had said, and she entered the café.

"Well," Red was thinking, "If that little girl belongs to Viola Haldeman, I can threaten her, and her momma will back off. I'll write her a note, tell her the little girl will disappear if she doesn't back off on contesting the deed."

Red waited until nearly midnight when the whole town was locked down. He picked up the lock on the front door and placed his note on the first table, just inside the door. He locked the door back and left, riding back to the Webber ranch.

Clawson waited two days and rode to Fredericksburg to the county clerk's office. "Is the court case still on for Danny Haldeman's deed dispute?" he asked.

"Yes, there's been no change in the court date," the clerk said.

"Damn," Red was thinking, "Either she did not find the note, or the little girl is not hers. If I go to court, I may land in jail. And, if they find out about Webber, I may get hung."

Red decided to hide across from the café in the alley as he had done before and just kill the woman when she closed that night. "Hell," he thought, "I've killed from ambush before." He waited for several hours, his hands sweaty. He had never killed a woman before, but he knew if this deal was going to work for him, it was something he had to do.

Viola closed and locked her café door. Red was squeezing on the trigger of his gun when some cowboys leaving the cantina fired a shot in the air, whooping and hollering. Red flinched at the noise and missed his shot, hitting the door jamb.

Viola must have jumped a foot, screamed and ran all the way home. She told Beacher the next morning that some cowboys shooting their guns off had nearly hit her. Beacher dug the bullet out from the door jamb.

"It's not a pistol ball," Beacher said. "This came out of an old 45/70, too much lead for a hand gun. I haven't seen one of them old rifles around for several years."

"What are you saying, Beacher?" Viola asked.

"I think someone shot at you with a rifle and missed," he told her. "It had to come from the alley across the street. Ted, you or Chuck watch that alley every night from now on."

Since Beacher was hanging around the café, he decided to make himself useful by sweeping the floor. While he was picking up the trash, he found Red's note. He read it to himself and sat down and looked around the room. Usually, Katy was around somewhere but he didn't see her. He asked Viola where Katy was.

"She said something about catching toad frogs for her fishing line," Viola told him. "That's all she talks about after you taught her how to fish."

"Where does she generally look?" Beacher asked.

"East of town by the river bank. There's some trees and grass and she told me there are a lot of toad frogs there, and she just wanted the small ones," Viola told him.

Beacher showed Viola the note. She read it and ran out of the door, headed toward the river. She ran all the way, and Beacher could not keep up with her. Katy was nowhere around. Beacher started looking the ground over and finally saw a spot where her tracks and a horse met before her tracks disappeared. Beacher decided that Red must have snatched her and rode off.

The Ranger followed the tracks but lost them in the river. "Looks like they're going downstream," he thought to himself. "I bet he's taking her to the Webber spread." Viola was getting hysterical and he tried to calm her down.

"Katy's a very smart girl," he told Viola. "She will escape if she can. You stay at the café, and me and the Youngers will see if we can track him."

Beacher and Viola went back into town and he rounded up his deputies. The three of them got their horses and some trail food, consisting of dried meat, bread and coffee. As he was getting ready to leave Beacher made the promise to Viola, "I will stay on his trail until I find Katy, and I'll kill the SOB."

The men rode the river's banks on both sides and never found where Red came out. They gave up and just rode to the Webber ranch, getting there after dark. Beacher asked the Younger brothers about the ranch house.

"Where would he hide a small child?" Beacher asked.

"The old house has a root cellar," Ted told him. "It's dark and very cold. When Jack's wife was alive she used it all the time, but Jack never opened it after she passed."

"Would Red know it's there?" asked Beacher.

"He can't miss it," Ted replied. "The door is right there in the kitchen."

Beacher asked, "Does it have another entrance?"

"Yeah, it does," Chuck responded. "It has a tunnel that went out into the garden area, but it's overgrown with morning glory. I couldn't see the entrance the last time I looked."

"Can you see the tunnel from inside?" the Ranger asked.

"No," Chuck said, "It's covered with a canvas door. If Red wasn't looking for it, he would never find it."

The men tied their horses on the back side of the barn where they couldn't be seen from the house. They sneaked around to the garden area. It sure was overgrown. It took Chuck a while to find the entrance to the cellar. Standing inside the tunnel, Beacher struck a match. It flared up and he used it to light a hand full of grass that was wound together. He cleared the spider webs and noticed that some were already gone. He looked at the floor and could see Katy's tracks, hers alone.

"Ted, she will head to the river and try to make her way back to town," Beacher said. "Follow her if you can. I aim to take care of Red Clawson right now. Chuck, you go around and cover the front door. I will go in this way and try to arrest him. If you hear shooting, bust the door in."

Katy was mad when Red picked her up. She kept hollering for him to put her down, but Red paid her no mind. Katy commenced to telling Red that she had a friend who was a Texas Ranger and that he was a very bad man to cross. She started telling him tall tales about Beacher, some Beacher had told her and some she just made up. That got Red to wondering just how much was true or not. He locked her in the root cellar as soon as he could. She was too little to kick the door down, and he didn't worry about another entrance.

Now, Katy was smart enough to know that a housewife would have matches and candles just inside the door. She began feeling around for them, lit a candle, and started looking around. There were a lot of spider webs. She had moved canvas back from several pantries before she found the tunnel and started down it. She finally came out in an overgrown garden, where she found some cucumbers and pulled one. She liked to eat them raw. Standing there in the garden, Katy could hear the river. She started walking toward the noise. Not too far from the ranch house she came upon the river bank. The river looked wider, but she decided to cross over. She knew town was on the west bank, and that she could just walk upstream and be home by sunup.

It was pretty smart thinking for a little girl, but the only thing wrong with her plans was that Katy did not know about the Llano and Colorado Rivers meeting south of Bluffton. Walking upstream was smart, but the fork put her on the Llano River heading more west than north. If Beacher did not figure out what she had done,

Katy was going to be ten miles further from home, and if she kept on walking, she was never going to find home.

Beacher found his way into the root cellar. He could see the light from a lantern around the edges of the door. He smelled bacon frying in a pan and bread in an oven maybe. It made his stomach grumble. He scratched on the door.

Red hollered. "Don't think I'm going to feed you! Just keep the hell quiet and thank your maker you're still alive!"

Beacher could tell where Clawson was standing by his voice. The Ranger kicked the door in and shot Red in the gut. Red hit the floor, spilling hot grease on himself, screaming and rolling all over the place. Beacher kicked the outlaw's gun across the floor. It had fallen out of Red's holster. Red finally realized what had happened to him.

"Man, get me to a doctor. You gut-shot me," the outlaw said.

"I intended to," Beacher said, "For kidnapping Katy."

"I didn't hurt her!" Red insisted.

"Were you going to feed her or just let her starve?" asked Beacher. Red made no comment, just stared at the Ranger.

"Tell me what happened to Danny Haldeman," Beacher said.

"Go to hell," Red replied.

"I'll get you to a doctor," said Beacher, "Just tell me about Haldeman."

Red tried to spit on the Ranger. Beacher shot the SOB in a kneecap, and the outlaw screamed again.

"Red, I can do this all night long," the Ranger offered, then shot him in the other kneecap. Red called Beacher things the lawman had never heard before.

Chuck had made his way inside and was standing in the kitchen. He picked up the skillet that still had some hot grease in the bottom of it and started dripping it on Red's head, one drop at a time.

Red was screaming, "I shot Haldeman and rolled him into the river, watched him float downstream!"

Beacher told Chuck to drag Clawson into the yard. There was no need in messing up the house any more than it was.

"Stay here until he's dead," Tolbert instructed. "I'm going to track Ted and Katy."

Beacher got his horse and rode to the river. He stopped and looked around. The moon was out, but not very bright. He shouted Katy's name as loud as he could, then listened but hearing nothing. Beacher was thinking, "What would Katy do? Follow the river on the east bank, or try to cross here?" The river didn't look deep and was very wide. He pondered on it for a while.

Beacher did see Ted's horse tracks on the east side, going north. He would find her unless Katy hid from him. He was sure that if Ted did not find her before reaching Bluffton, he would turn around and come back this way. Beacher crossed the river, dismounted and walked upriver, looking for a wet spot along the bank, sure that Katy would leave one.

Chuck dragged Red out of the house and into the yard. He was thinking, "I don't want this buzzard buried on Jack's ranch. I'm going to drag him down to the river, and if he's still alive when I get there, I'm just going to roll his backside in and let him drown." Chuck tied a rope around Clawson's boots, mounted his horse, and dragged the outlaw down to the river. The man was still alive when Chuck got there. He rolled the man into the river and Red tried to swim, then went under. Chuck followed him downstream for a long way, then rode out into the river and put a slug in his head. "Good enough for the SOB," Chuck said.

Chapter 6

Beacher found no trace of Katy crossing the river but rode up the west bank anyway. He walked his horse for close to a mile, figuring if Katy came this way, he was close to her.

Katy heard the horse walking in the gravel along the bank. Thinking it was the same man who kidnapped her, she hid in the water's edge among some reeds. Fast water was making some noise. Katy hid until the rider passed by, came out of the water and started walking north, or so she thought.

Ted rode all the way to Bluffton and stopped at the café. Viola had not opened and was just sitting on the boardwalk, red-eyed. She asked Ted about Katy. He told the mother all he knew, that Katy had escaped, and he was following her along the east bank of the river.

"If she's not here, then I must have passed her along the way," Ted said. "I need to go back and find her."

"I'm going with you," Viola said. She walked to the livery barn and came out with a buggy, already hitched up. She started for the river, crossed and headed south. They met Chuck and stopped to ask about Katy.

"No sign of her on this side of the river," Chuck said. He told Ted and Viola about Beacher shooting Red. "I finished him off, let him drown in the river floating south. I did not want him buried on Jack's ranch."

All three of them went back to the Webber ranch and on west to the river, pondering what to do.

Ted asked Viola, "Does Katy know there are two rivers here?"

"What do you mean?" she asked.

Ted told her about the Llano River running into the Colorado close to a mile north of where they were.

'No," Viola said. "And Katy doesn't know about the Llano. I've never seen it myself."

"We need to go back to the north fork, cross over, and follow it back to town," Ted suggested. "If we don't find Katy by then, she crossed and is following the Llano River, and it goes northwest."

They crossed and rode all the way back to Bluffton but found no Katy. Viola was getting very upset.

Ted, trying to calm her down, said, "Let's go back to the fork and up the east side of the Llano. If she crosses it, we will find her. I'll bet money Beacher is on the west side looking for her."

Beacher rode all the way to Llano, a small town on the river bank. No Katy. He turned around and started back, trying to figure out just how far the little girl could walk in a day. It was getting dark, so he stopped in a clearing. He could see nearly a half mile. He built a big fire and gathered up all the dead wood he could find. It was close to midnight when Viola and the Younger boys crossed the river to his fire. Beacher told Chuck and Ted to keep it going all night, figuring that if Katy was around, she would come to it.

Tolbert cut some bank poles, set out some hooks, and made coffee. Everyone was asleep when Beacher heard Katy in the water trying to pull in a big catfish.

"You want some help, Katy?" he asked.

"No, but you can cook him. I'm hungry," she said. Katy ate the whole fish by herself. Viola was asleep, and Katy just crawled up next to her momma and went to sleep herself.

During the next two weeks, both land dispute claims were out of court. Beacher signed off on them and told Chuck and Ted that if no relatives filed on the land in ten years, they could consider the land theirs. Chuck said he was going to get a marker for Jacks grave and Ted agreed. Beacher showed Viola Danny's place and she said she would talk to Ted about it. Tolbert had noticed they were getting kind of friendly and was betting that they would work something out. He told Katy goodbye and left Bluffton.

The Ranger rode to Fredericksburg and wired Austin that Red Clawson was dead, the land deeds were settled, and he was still drifting around some. He did not get out the door before he got a wire back.

"Drift out to Fort Stockton," the wire read. "Someone around there selling guns to Mescalero Apache Indians.

All the rifles found with dead Indians have been old military guns. Find out source." Late in the day Beacher found a boarding house with a bath. "My lucky day," he thought. "It'll probably be the last bath I see for a while."

Beacher left for Fort Stockton early the next morning. The trip took him two weeks. He saw a lot of brush country. Tolbert never knew there was that many cedar trees in Texas. He had several encounters with long-horned cattle. Joe Horton Tolbert had told him about them, but he didn't believe there could be so many of them. And, Joe was right about the old bulls being meaner than hell.

Beacher arrived at Fort Stockton. It was mess time when he went to the headquarters. The Commanding Officer was a Colonel Herring. Tolbert was thinking, "I'm going to have some fun with this idiot." He introduced himself, "I'm Beacher Tolbert, Texas Ranger, and I need to stay at the Fort for a while, on assignment, but I cannot tell you why."

"Okay," Herring said, "I've got an empty quarter you can use. Let's go to mess."

Beacher was sitting at a table with Colonel Herring and two other men and asked about Sergeant Joe Horton.

Colonel Herring was the first to answer, "He's out on scouting detail."

One of the other men, a Captain, said, "I've been here two years and I've never met him."

"Well," Herring said, "He likes it out there."

"Well," Beacher said, "I need to talk with him and a Captain Lewis about a matter back east of here. When will he be back at the Fort? I need to hang around and talk to him."

Colonel Herring was squirming around in his chair. Beacher was thinking to himself, "This Colonel Herring knows Joe is not here and he's collecting Joe's salary. Probably Captain Lewis', also. I need to find out who is charge. Hell, if Herring is that much of a crook, he may be the one selling old military guns to the Mescalero Apache." It was known only to Beacher that Joe Horton, a sergeant at the time, shot Captain Lewis and rolled his body into a burning Indian wikiup, and deserted on account of Lewis killing an Indian child. Joe had decided that if the Army was going to kill children he did not belong there, and just left. He changed his name from Horton to Tolbert, went from a third cousin to a first cousin. Joe had told Beacher all of this after he joined the Texas Rangers.

Tolbert stayed around for a week before Herring told him that Horton would be in to see him "tomorrow." "Wonder how he's going to pull this off?" Beacher thought, "Because I know for a fact that Horton is with a Hitch Westmoreland chasing a bank robber down in Mexico, using a young boy name Poncho Villa as a guide. That's about two hundred miles from here."

At mess the next day, Colonel Herring showed up with a young recruit. Herring said, "This is Sergeant Joe Horton." They sat down at Beacher's bench and he never said a word until he was through.

Beacher stood up and said, "Let's go for a ride." Colonel Herring was tagging along when Tolbert stopped and looked at him. "In private. We don't need you to go with us."

Herring insisted.

Beacher stopped and stared at him. "You know your fort is on Texas land. If you would like to keep it here, me and Sergeant Joe Horton are going for a ride alone." Colonel Herring stamped back inside the mess hall.

They rode out nearly two miles before Beacher stopped, thinking to himself, "This kid is dumber than a box of dirt." Tolbert said, "Sergeant, I know your name is not Horton. What is it?"

"Miles," he said.

Beacher asked why he was impersonating an officer of the US Army.

"Colonel Herring told me to," Miles answered.

"Man, the Army could have you in front of a firing squad. You want to go there?" Beacher asked.

"No," he replied.

"Well, you need to tell me everything you know about this Colonel Herring."

Miles told Beacher that he and two other new recruits had just arrived that morning.

"Do they know your real name?" Beacher asked.

"No, we never exchanged names," Miles replied. "We just rode in on the stage together."

"Good," the Ranger said. "So, from now on you're Sergeant Joe Horton. Colonel Herring is going to ask you what we talked about. Tell him nothing. Just say that it's private and leave it there. Now, I'm going to tell you something that may save your life, and you can tell Herring this if you want to. I'm Texas Ranger Beacher Tolbert. You're my third cousin and I haven't seen you in twenty or so years. That would make you only around five the last time we met. That's all you can tell him. Now, this is a secret, and you can't tell anyone. Someone in Fort Stockton is selling old military guns to the Mescalero Indians. I need you to work with me since Colonel Herring has already drawn you into it. And, since he has made you a Sergeant, he can't back down for as long as I'm around. So, from now on, you're Sergeant Joe Horton.

Chapter 7

"I am going to like this," Miles thought. "And I'm going to rub it in Colonel Herring's face all I can." Then it dawned on him, "What's going to happen when Ranger Tolbert leaves? Maybe I need to keep a low profile and see if I can help find out who's selling guns to the Mescalero Indians."

Colonel Herring was mad as hell at himself. "Now I've got to pay a Sergeant Joe Horton out of my pocket," he was thinking. "It's going to cost me a lot of money until I can get rid of him. And, just who is this Ranger to come in here and ask about a Sergeant that's been dead five years. I'm drawing his salary and still have him on payroll. Hell, I can always send Miles on an Indian raiding party. I've got a private, Darwin, who will take care of him for me, and it won't cost me anything.

******

Beacher stayed at Fort Stockton for over sixty days before ever seeing any Indians. Two came to the fort, had a pow-wow with Herring in private, and left mad. Beacher could tell because they were whooping and hollering in Spanish, used a lot of bad words. He played like he didn't understand them. He figured for as long as he was around, Herring or whoever it was selling the guns, would not be selling them if he was there.

A town was beginning to grow around Fort Stockton so Beacher decided to move. A new, two-story hotel had just gone up with a cantina that had some dancing girls. Beacher got a room upstairs that faced the Fort's main gate, and he could see a long way. The evening sun was at his back. He had told Miles to keep his eyes open, to let Beacher know if a wagon left loaded with anything that had no army escort.

"Hell," Beacher was thinking, "If Herring was selling old fire arms to the Mescalero, he could not do it by himself. There has to be someone else helping him. I never saw a Colonel drive a wagon before."

Tolbert hadn't been in town but a day before Miles came by the cantina to see him. The Sergeant walked by Beacher's table and dropped a note, written in Spanish. Beacher translated as he read the note to himself, "A wagon with two soldiers will leave the fort at daybreak headed to Monahan's. Driver, Private Miles, along with a Private Darwin. Some old guns in the floor, covered with a tarp."

Beacher was thinking it would be hard to trail the wagon without being seen. That night he rode on to Monahan's ahead of them and found a hideout. One where he could see a long way and watch for them. It sounded like a good plan at the time. He'd left for Monahan's that night, learning that it was just a trading post south of some sand hills. There was a small, natural lake and a lot of trees. A natural place for an Indian camp. He didn't expect the wagon to get there until the next day.

Tolbert made camp in some hills atop one of the mesas. He built a fire, hidden in a buffalo wallow, and made his evening meal of coffee, bacon, and fried bread in the left-over grease. He rolled up in his tarp after the fire went down. It was a quiet night and Beacher slept well, until something woke him up. The fire was going again, quite large. He jumped straight up when at what he saw by the fire. It scared the hell out of Tolbert and he damned near had a runaway.

An old Indian woman, very short and bent over with nothing on but her hair that hung down around her legs. It looked as if it had never been combed in her life. Solid grey in color, it looked eerie in the fire light. She turned and looked at Beacher, one tooth in the middle of her mouth. She was holding the skillet and was licking it clean.

"I've heard of them," Beacher thought. "Haunts, their called. But I never expected to encounter one." He had heard they were attracted by your fire, never bothering anything, just eat what you left and then leave. Indian's would leave their old ones behind when they moved camp. If they had nobody to care for them, the tribe just left them to nature. She stayed all night sitting by the fire with Beacher in the shadows.

At daylight the Ranger broke camp and left. The Haunt was still sitting there. He hoped he would never encounter another one. Beacher thought it was a bad omen, that it meant someone you knew was going to die.

Tolbert stayed in the hills. He found a spot where he could see the trading post. There was a wagon in the distance. The driver was taking his time. When it got within a mile of Beacher's location, he could see there was only one person in the wagon seat. It was hard to tell if it was Miles or Private Darwin. He watched as the driver and trading post owner unloaded the wagon. Beacher could tell there was still something wrapped up in the wagon box, and decided it was Miles. Beacher figured Darwin would have himself a drink and spend the night. There weren't many times a Private could drink all night and get away with it.

Beacher rode a long way around the trading post and got there just after dark. He had three sticks of dynamite in his saddle bag. He tied them together in a bundle and placed them at the rear of a back wall. There was a big rock there and he stuck the dynamite between the rock and the building, near the middle. The Ranger found a can of kerosene and set it on top of the rock. He lit a long fuse cord and walked around to the front, nearly a hundred feet from the doors and waited.

Boom! The ceiling fell in, walls blew out, and some pieces hit Beacher. The whole thing caught fire. Somebody was trying to crawl out. The Ranger waited for him to stand up, then gut-shot him. It was Private

Darwin. The private was the only one to crawl out, and the whole building burned to the ground.

Beacher took Darwin's gun away from him and threw him in the wagon with Miles. He tied his horse on the back and headed to Fort Stockton. It looked as if Darwin had killed Miles right after leaving the fort. Darwin lasted half the way back to Fort Stockton, complaining all the way and begging for water. Tolbert didn't feel for the man, just let him die a slow death.

Beacher turned the team loose just outside of the fort, knowing they would find their way home. Horses always do. "Let Colonel Herring try and figure out what happened," he thought.

Tolbert rode out of Fort Stockton the next day. He saw two new graves, a Private Darwin and a Private Miles, killed in an Indian raid stamped on both markers. "Well," Beacher thought, "I guess Sergeant Joe Horton is still alive. I need to do something about that."

Beacher wired Austin and told his captain, "Colonel Herring was the person selling guns to the Indians. Can't prove it, but Herring is collecting payroll on one Captain Lewis killed in Indian battle along with Sergeant Joe Horton, nearly five years past. Both men are still on pay roster and Colonel Herring, along with paymaster, have got to be the guilty parties. Send warrant for arrest of Colonel Herring and acting paymaster ASAP."

Tolbert woke up that night from a nightmare about the damned Indian woman with all that hair, holding his skillet and licking it clean. *"Need to throw it away and get me a new one,"* he thought.

Chapter 8

Texas Ranger Beacher Tolbert rode out to Fort Stockton armed with an arrest warrant for Colonel Herring and the paymaster. He found Master Sergeant Mann and told him, privately, what was going to happen and that he needed to take charge of the fort. Beacher told Mann to just tell Colonel Herring to meet Ranger Tolbert at the stockade, that he would be waiting on him.

Tolbert walked to the paymaster's office, Sergeant Honeycutt. He asked the sergeant how long he had been in charge of the payroll.

"Five years," Honeycutt said. Beacher handed him his arrest warrant. Honeycutt sat there with his mouth open. Seeing he was not armed, Beacher gave the man a choice, walk to the stockade or be dragged.

The Ranger was locking the man up as Colonel Herring arrived with Master Sergeant Mann. Beacher handed the warrant to the Master Sergeant and said, "You need to read it out loud."

"Colonel Herring, Commanding Officer at Fort Stockton," Mann read the warrant, "You are under arrest for theft of Army payroll. One Captain Lewis and one Sergeant Joe Horton, killed in an Indian raid over three years past, and kept on the Army payroll. You can defend yourself at your Court Martial." Mann stripped Herring of his rank and locked him up.

Beacher left and found the Sergeant in charge of burial detail. He had Miles' marker changed to Sergeant Joe Horton and a grave in question of three years old to Captain Lewis. He signed off on the duty roster and wrote in the log, "After a long and weary investigation, unquestionably correct men are in their graves. Signed, Texas Ranger Beacher Tolbert."

As Beacher rode away from Fort Stockton his mind began to wander. "Think I'll ride over to Pecos. I heard a judge over there thinks he's the only law in Texas."

Tolbert stayed two weeks in and around Judge Roy Bean's saloon, and watched the man hold several trials. There was even a mock hanging. The rope was too long, and the judge knew it was. He sprung the trap door, the man hit the ground, got up and ran off. It scared him enough that Beacher bet he never wanted to come before Judge Bean again.

Tolbert watched Bean give away fines he collected during the day to widow women at night. The Judge did not know Beacher was watching him. Bean had a strange sense of humor.

Ranger Tolbert never told Judge Bean who he was, just watched the man. Bean had no jail cells, so he would stake bad men out in front of the saloon. Generally, a day was enough punishment for anybody.

Beacher decided Roy Bean was the right man for the job in this lawless part of Texas. His wire to Austin said,

"Judge Roy Bean is the law west of the Pecos. For now, let's leave him alone. Long ride, but I'm headed to El Paso. May never get another chance to see this part of Texas."